Donald's Terrible, No Good Christmas

Written by Jonathan Brown
Illustrated by Walt Gabriel

On Christmas Eve all snuggled in bed, Donald dreamed of walls in his head.

Then he awoke with a knock-knock on the door. Who could this be? What is this for?

He crept down the stairs with ease as can be.

Who's here?
He needed to see.

When he came to the door,
he opened to peek.
He felt the cold air
rush over his cheek.

Why it was Stormy and Karen with frowns on their faces. "Come in, come in!" He said. "This is the finest of places!"

The women obliged and walked in the door.
The Donald, you see, did not want a war.

They walked and they talked,
they talked and they walked.
In hushed little voices,
debated his choices.

"Come hither come here,
this path is clear!
Step into this room."
He whispered so soon.

They stepped in the dark
and followed this shark.

As they walked in, they noticed his grin.

He then slammed the door,
it was no small chore.

"Haha, don't you see!
You'll never get me!
Christmas is near,
I have nothing to fear!"

"You rascal you rat!
We'll get you at that!"

He walked down the hall all cheery and glee. He thought to himself they'll never catch me!

Then the phone rang with a soft pang.

"Papa, Papa," the voice tried to say.
"They've caught me in a lie on this day today!"

For who could it be?
The oldest of three.

"Don't worry my son," Donald explained, "you've nothing to fear, your pardons right here!"

Donald hung up the phone, this crisis prevented.

"Gosh darn these feds,"
The Donald, he vented.

He strolled to the tree
as proud as can be.
The presents were there
all snuggled with care.

One for Melania that's it, not one more. Then two for young Barron, he got his wish. Not one, but two fish! The last of the presents oh my oh me, this person got three! They towered so high, that they touched the sky. A note was there for this person to share.

"For Putin, my friend, with love these I send."

Wrapped up all inside, democracy was gifted with pride.

"Well done" thought Donald, "my goal is complete."

I've sold out democracy, which is no small feat."

Then the clock chimed,
for now, it was time.
Christmas was here,
what a great year!

Melania and Barron walked down with poise when all of a sudden there was a loud noise.

The roof, could it be?
Santa, we'll see!

Footsteps above,
Donald pushed with a shove.
Down the chimney, they came,
not Santa or fame.

It was Mueller and friends
with warrants in hand.
This was not what,
poor Donald had planned!

Donald, oh my,
he scattered and ran.
He yelled, "Giuliani,
start the van!"

He opened the door
to find a surprise.
He couldn't believe
his two little eyes.
For Stormy and Karen escaped
don't you see,
just in time to stop
this crime spree.

Donald met his fate
not a moment too late.
Off to prison, no key,
that's all that could be.

For Donald today,
this terrible day,
was his last free Christmas
some people say.

Check out more art by Walt Gabriel!

Instagram: @waltgabriel.art
Email: waltgabrielart@gmail.com

ISBN
978-1948569262

Made in the USA
Middletown, DE
09 December 2018